Parallel Universe Bar

By Abigail Blanchard

Chapter 1

The doors open at Savior's Bar. It is one of, if not the best bar in Ghafterlift city.

The owner is a man by the name of Rein, who has a mostly bald head but with brown splotches of hair, and chocolate brown eyes. He currently polishing some of his silverware in the bar. He is one of the few people working at this hour, because there is still light in the day, and the main drinkers haven't arrived yet. There is another person at the bar at this hour working, with him. He goes by the name of Selvester. Rein looks over at Selvester, who is busy taking an order from a customer.

Rein didn't know what to think of Selvester. Selvester has gorgeous yellow hair, and beautiful sliver eyes, but has mysterious scars on his arms from an incident, that Selvester refuses to talk about. He is one of the first people to join, and was quite frankly a very good bartender. The bar itself wouldn't have gotten very far without him. However, as time goes on Selvester starts acting strange toward Rein, and it is hard to pin-point why.

The reason why it is so odd is because Selvester is a very quiet chap, and usually keeps to himself. He is also very monotone. Rarely, Rein has seen Selvester in a dimeter other than his calm usual self, but there is still something off about him, especially around Rein himself. Selvester kind of acts like there is a bunch of butterflies in his stomach, whenever he talks to Rein. Rein isn't sure what it is, but he doesn't think it is necessarily bad, just weird. Rein's closest conclusion is that Selvester has a small crush on him, but that is impossible. Rein, in his own mind, is unattractive loser. He's most likely misinterrupting Selvester's behavior.

After this small thought tangent, Rein goes back to polishing. Suddenly, the doorbell rings, and someone steps inside. Rein looks up and smiles. It is one of his favorite regulars, Niko.

Niko has black hair and green shimmering eyes; he is also an off-duty police officer, who is currently recovering from losing his arm. He has cheerful and friendly personality, and he never drinks at the bar, but instead buys some food and talks to other people. Rein gave him the nickname, 'Stranger Driver', because of the amount of times Niko has driven some rando home, and usually never gets anything in return.

Niko sits on one of the stools in front of Rein, and starts up a conversation.

"Hey-a, Rein!" Niko immediately says. Selvester's face changes for a second, but then goes back to his normal uninterested look.

"Hi. The usual?" Rein asks.

"Yep!" Niko replies. Rein tells Selvester, who was just done with his own order, to deliver Niko's burger and fries for him. Selvester goes through a door, and comes back with an already prepared burger and fries. Selvester gives it to Niko and carries on with his duties, without saying a word.

"Thank you!" Niko tells Selvester as the bartender walks away. Niko then turns to Rein and says, "Wow, that was quick."

"Well, you're usually here at a certain time, and a certain date so making a fresh batch is usually quite easy," Rein replies.

"Heh. You really like your regulars," Niko says.

"Only the favorite one," Rein replies.

"Yeah, I'm pretty sure the 'cultists' aren't that high on your list, since you're so sure one of them stole some booze," Niko tells Rein.

If Rein couldn't understand Selvester, he definitely didn't understand the cultists. Rein nicknamed them the cultists because they always showed up in disguises and usually, they were long robes. The disguises were pretty good, in that fact he couldn't see their faces. In the beginning, he thought they were all the same person. Then he thought it was the same person but with a personality disorder. Then after seeing double, he concludes that yes, they are different people, which makes it very hard to ban them after one of them stole some alcohol, when they are denied drinks, because they refuse to show any id! In Rein's opinion, that behavior is very strange. "Why go to a bar, when you can't show any id?" Rein always thinks to himself whenever he starts

thinking about the cultists.

Niko breaks his train of thought by saying, "Have you seen

any of them lately? I'm sure we'll catch that criminal!"

"Hmm, last week I did. One of them asked specially for you.

I told him you didn't work here, but I didn't tell him that you

were a regular," Rein says to him. Niko gets an uncomfortable

look on his face.

"Oh no. Please don't say one of the cultists is part of the

Coven Clan!" Niko replies upsettably.

"They might. The Coven Clan has a lot of members, and

they could have spies. I also never seen any those cultists' faces

before, but those chances are low. So, I'm sure you'll be safe!"

"Thanks that's very helpful. It's not like they cost me an arm!

Oh wait," Niko replies in a 'really' tone. A moment of silence

pasts. The Coven Clan is the name of a mafia group that uses a lot of 'religious symbols' in their clothing, weapons, face paint, and even what they leave behind after their raids. They were also very weird mafia group. One example is their symbols. They are not the regular, Christian, Egyptian, Aztec, Ant, or Greek symbols, but literal ones and zeros. Like the numbers that make up computer programs, and videogames. Rein is also pretty sure they do witchcraft, and are a cult. No sane criminal organization would put **that** much thought in their style.

Everybody knows that they are trouble, but Rein's sure they won't go after a random police officer, right? Then, why was that cultist member looking for him? Maybe they were angrier about Niko stopping their raid against Blatant Labs, than Rein thought, which puts a knot in Rein's stomach.

"Wanna know something that scares me?" Niko says in a hushed tone, which snaps Rein back to reality.

"Y-Yeah?"

"The Coven Clan was able to make me lose an arm, but…

I'm pretty sure that's nothing on what they are truly capable of. I

mean, I'm pretty sure if my partner Richey didn't pull me out of

the way…" Niko grows silent, and it infects Rein as well.

Rein did see the news report of the incident on his tv. So

many civilians and police officers lost their lives that day. Rein

shivers thinking about if he ever joined the police force instead of

making his own business, would he have ended up dead? No.

Niko, and many others went through it and lived. It wasn't a

granted 100% survival, but it was better than a 100% death rate.

Sensing the awkwardness of talking about Coven Clan, the

two immediately switched topics and continued talking well into

the evening, even when more costumers and more employees

show up. At one point in the conversation, Niko tells Rein about

him thinking about not getting a regular prosthetic hand, but

instead getting a gun for hand. Rein rolls his eyes at this, and is mostly sure Niko was joking. Mostly. At the end, Niko pays for the food, and begins to leave.

"Don't forget to go to bed! You have employees for a reason!" Niko tells Rein, before he leaves. Rein, not taking this advice, continues working until midnight, which Rein is greatly unsatisfied with, because he wants to continue working until 2:am, but all the regulars and the employees knows of his workaholic personality, so after much convincing and pushing Rein finally goes up stairs to sleep.

The bar has another purpose besides being a bar. It is Rein's home. He sleeps in the attic, which has a comfy bed, a nightstand, a drawer, a framed picture of a 5 star review he received, and a small window that looks out to the city. Rein goes to bed, and besides his worries that he didn't do enough today, he falls asleep rather quickly.

Chapter 2

HONK! Rein immediately jumps out of bed, and looks over to see a horn floating in mid-air. If that didn't scare him for the mere impossibility of it, the weird looking elephant that is standing on her hindlegs did.

The elephant appears to be human like, and that her feet and hands seem to be in the shape of human's feet and hands. She also seems to be around 7ft tall, but that isn't the weirdest bit of it. She has 4 arms instead of two, and green and yellow butterfly wings on her back. Her shoes look to be sandals, and is wearing some Roman robes that appear to be made out of some green fabric. She also has a golden pin on that robe, which has a black outline of a ghost on it.

"About time you woke up!" The creature spits. The floating horn disappears into nothingness.

"W-who are you?!" Rein asks flabbergasted, "What are you!?"

"My name is $Yio*," The creature replies, but then says something that Rein couldn't quite understand.

"What?" Rein asks.

"Oh right, there isn't a word in your dictionary for my name," The creature tells him exhaustively, "Just call me um, Susie! I think that's a good dorange name,"

"Why are you here?" Rein asks.

"Um, the question you should be asking is 'why am I here' like for you, not me, but the reason is that I need you to be my detective," Susie replies.

"What are you talking about?" Rein asks, but then looks outside of his window. Instead of seeing a bustling night in the city, he sees a black void of emptiness, filled with big shiny bubbles, that look like they each contain a galaxy. Rein faints, because of the shock.

"Oh great!" Susie says, and a new horn is created right next to Rein's face and is blown. He jolts awake.

"Stop that!" Rein shouts and pushes the horn away. The horn acts like gravity doesn't exist and floats away into the air like sturdy bubble, but once its losses its momentum it freezes. Rein gets up on his feet and watches the new horn disappear.

"How did you do that?"

"Well, you see. I'm basically your god. Well, I don't feel like a god per se, but I did create you so," Rein looks at her funny.

"Well, I am a god because both me and the theoretical version of God can create matter and destroy it without consequences! Well, it's a bit more complicated than that, but right now that's not important. Right now, you should focus that the god of your world, wants you to do something for them,"

"O-ok," Rein says, but everything is happening so fast he has no idea what to think, "So, why does… **God**… want me to do something for them?"

"I go by she/her pronouns, but let's just say I want to do an experiment. Let me tell you a story. Once upon a time, there was this person called, um let's say… Sloth, because that is what they are, anyways, they own a world kind of similar, actually not at all similar to yours, but what matters is that you have a world, and this one was a different breed of world. Now the world itself is called Storium, and it wasn't half bad. It was actually a delightful one. However, there are these *creatures*, that you guys call demons, but are actually called preditions. It isn't that important, actually keep calling them demons. They get pretty annoyed by

that!"

"Um…"

"Oh, right! Sorry! They were created by some mad

individual, to destroy all of our hard work by convincing you

doranges to sell your soul to it. Another thing I should mention, is

that perditions are…messy. Anyone involved with the deal gets

their soul stolen. Their soul can be saved by the opposite of the

demon's savior, except the one who made the deal in the first

place. Get me? Anyways, one of Storium's doranges sold their

soul, and the usual happened, until… the end. That demon went

back on its end of the bargain and conquers the whole world!

Which, like never happened before! Do you know what Sloth

did? For context, our responsibility to our worlds is to protect

them, and to make sure the worlds don't descend into chaos!

Sloth did **nothing. Didn't even care**! They just let their creations have their souls taken, and did nothing. They left it alone for so long, that the doranges made the perdition their god, and the main part of their religion! (Like what happen here, but on worse scale) Without even knowing that this creature is a horrible, horrible nightmare! However, what no one expected was for that perdition to be killed… by a dorange. Those creatures haven't been killed that way before… That got us curious. Could a dorange get rid of their own demons? So, when a very bad perdition problem appeared, instead of it letting it play out or simply getting rid of it, I decided to make it an experiment, because I'm the only Orchifly smart enough for the job. I want to see if people like **you** can get rid of one, or at least figure something out. So, you are going to go downstairs and act like an <u>undercover</u> detective, and interrogate the suspects, in secret. Don't worry, I'll help you if it gets rough by resetting everyone's memories, and bringing them back, if it ever comes to that,"

Rein blinks. He's a bit overwhelmed by Susie's monologue. After taking a moment to recover, he says, "I don't understand. Isn't the only way to kill a perdition was by another perdition or a savior? I can't do that! Besides, why me?"

"One, who says you are going to kill it? You're just pointing it out. Besides, we aren't allowed to kill other's creations. Those things are just a very irritating loophole. Second, I might not know the context of the deal, but I know that it involves parallel timelines of the world I created, and all the suspects who could have done it; have hopped timelines, have all ended up in your timeline at some point, and met you," Susie replies.

"Th-Then why didn't I know them?" Rein wonders to himself out loud, "I would assume I would notice people who aren't from my timeline…D-did I eat something funny?"

"Wow. You actually don't know?! The people you named the 'cultists' are actually alternate versions of yourself," Susie answers, "Thought you already knew this already, and you didn't eat anything funny. I just teleported you here" A moment of silence passes.

"Ok, now this is way too much to take in," Rein responds.

"Welp, I don't care. Good luck!" Susie replies and suddenly disappears.

Chapter 3

After a moment of processing what in the world just

happened, Rein begins to descend his staircase and goes into the

bar part of 'his' house. The copy of his bar is mostly similar to his

own; however, there is some strange looking ivy that is growing

almost everywhere. All the leaves have holes in them to make it

look like some sort of amalgamation of eyes. Rein shivers a bit,

and stops looking at the plant. There were also no entrance/exit

doors, but a new door that led somewhere. Rein couldn't see the door that led to the kitchen at the angle he is at, so he didn't know

if it was gone, or not.

He sees the front of the bar is currently occupied, with you

guessed it! Himself. There were six of himself, actually.

The first one that catches Rein's eye first is a Rein with police

clothing. The Rein looks like he's very sad, and reserved.

Something bad probably happen to him recently. "Could it be

enough to make a deal with a perdition?" Rein thinks to himself.

The Rein next to him is wearing casual clothing, but seems

to be on edge. This Rein is very close to another Rein who is

wearing professional scientist clothing, who seems very happy.

"That one that is on the edge. Is he hiding something, like

per say, a perdition deal? Then there's the other one with the

science clothing. Did he make a deal with a perdition to expand

his knowledge? Don't scientists do questionable things to learn something new. Wait is Susie a scientist?" Rein again thinks to

himself.

The next Rein over, is wearing a garbageman's uniform. He

seems happy, although a bit bittersweet.

"…Okay I've got nothing, which probably means he's the

murder. Since it's always the last person you expect,"

The last Rein that is in the front bar section, is a Rein with

dirty, ripped up clothing. He is far away from the group, like the

cop Rein is, and is as depressed or more so than him.

"He looks like he has had a hard life…Not that I could

blame him," Rein grabs his own arm and applies pressure to it, as

he sympathizes with the other version of himself "Maybe he

made the deal so that his luck would change,"

All the Reins, except one of course, were looking up at the

counter. It is because there is one there that is standing on the

counter with clothing that reminds Rein of the Coven Clan. He looks like he's telling the rest of them something. Rein almost yells at him to get off the counter, when he sees that this Rein **is** wearing clothing from the Coven Clan and is most likely a member. Rein starts tiptoeing back upstairs, when *Creek* Thanks to that, he is soon spotted by the Coven Clan Rein, and the others.

"Hey! Get back over here!" The Coven Clan Rein yells at him. Rein decides to book it up stairs.

"G-go after him!" One of the Reins, most likely Coven Clan Rein shouts. Rein (the one who owns the bar) runs into the attic and frantically tries to lock the door. However, this isn't Savior's Bar, and when Rein locks the door, the lock disappears with a voice that sounds exactly like Susie that says, "No,". In response, Rein grabs the drawer in the room, and puts it in front of the door while shouting back, "NO!". A loud bang against the door is heard. The cabinet is successful.

Unfortunately, for Rein, Susie needs him to meet them, and the drawer disappears, with another, "No,". The door swings open, and three Reins enter. None of them were the Coven Clan one. It is the scientist one, the garbageman one, and the cop one.

"S-stay back!" Rein shouts trying to find something to defend himself with.

"Calm down!" The garbageman Rein tries to tell him.

"N-no! You're Coven Clan! You're evil alternate versions me!" Rein shouts back.

"WHAT! NO! YUCK!" The cop Rein replies like Rein just offended him. The other two look almost as offended.

"No, no, no! Only one of us are Coven Clan, and Mob promises he won't hurt you!" The scientist Rein replies, "And… that's not Scout's thing"

"M-Mob?" Rein asks.

"Oh, that's new! We all were summoned here one at a time, and I thought that only timeline hoppers were being summoned here! Fascinating, but now I have to go back to square one on why we were summoned here…unless" The scientist Rein monologues, "Are you the bartender Rein?"

"I…what?" Rein asks.

"Let me explain it," The garbageman Rein says, "You see we are timeline hoppers, and we've been visiting this one timeline's bar, Savior's Bar. A Rein is the one who owns it, and um…are you that Rein?"

"No…" Rein says then remembers why he's here and he doesn't want to invoke god's wrath, "I mean! Y-yes. So, you're the um cultists. Huh, there's a lot more of you, than I thought there were,"

"My theory is saved! And it also explains why he doesn't know our codenames," Scientist Rein says.

"Codenames? Also please don't jump topics. I'm still recovering from the shock," Rein asks.

"Well, you see-" The scientist Rein begins.

"Actually, let me explain it," the garbageman Rein interrupts, "So, we are all named, Rein, and well it's kind of confusing if we all just used our real names. So, we gave each other nicknames to call each other. Mines Trash, cause I'm a garbageman. That's Dr. Fully," Trash points to the scientist Rein, "And he believes he's the first Rein, but he also says there's infinite number of Reins so who knows. He also made the timeline hoppers in the first place. The other one," Trash then points to the police officer, "Is Cop, because you guess it! A police officer,"

"Ok…" Rein says. Of course, they gave each other nicknames. Rein always gave his regulars nicknames. Why wouldn't alternate versions of himself not do the same?

"I. Ok. So, I don't know anything about alternate versions of my timeline or alternate myselfs. I mean, I just learned about it today," Rein asks.

"Huh, how did you learn about us. Cause I'm pretty sure we were all summoned here on the exact same day, and we weren't able to travel to different timelines, or else we could have gotten out of here already, so, how did you learn about us?" Dr. Fully asks.

"Well, it's because, ow!" Rein stammers. A little yellow rat comes up out of Rein's collar. Dr. Fully screams, while the others laugh at him.

"Sorry, about him. He hates rats," Trash laughs while speaking.

"Oh no! The rat is going to thaw your hard work away!" Cop tells Dr. Fully sarcastically.

"IT WILL! I ALMOST LOST MY JOB, BECAUSE OF THOSE IMPS!" Dr. Fully screeches. While the others were distracted, the rat actually spoke to Rein.

"Hey, Rein," the rat whispers to him, "Don't freak out."

It took all of Rein's courage not to and it also took the same amount of courage not to faint, "W-What! This has to be a fever dream!" Rein whispers back, "*Pause* Great now I'm going to have to skip work because of it…Maybe if I sit down-,"

"Unfortunately, it isn't. Ok, so um. $-I mean Susie. Doesn't want you to tell anyone about the deal, and she thinks you might need help. Just say one of them blew their cover, but then that one ran away," the rat whispers Rein. Rein feels guilt weighing on him because he almost blew his mission. Even if he's being forced to do this, he doesn't want to prove his parents right that he is a useless mistake. It doesn't help that this person is literally God. Rein then gives this false information to the others.

"Huh, I wonder who that could be?" Dr. Fully says.

"Could be Trash…" Cop says.

"HEY!" Trash says.

While the Reins argue, the bartender Rein realizes the rat on his shoulder hasn't disappeared yet.

"Ok…are you leaving now?" Rein asks the rat.

"I don't want to disappear, and I'm pretty sure it is against the Orchiflies' rules. So, how about I be your, Watson?" the rat whispers.

"Ok…what's your name?" Rein asks.

"Don't have one, how about you give me a name!" The rat says.

"Hm, how about Angel? Angel Shot." Rein says.

"Ah. Well, it's my fault, because I was the one who I asked. So, that's… now my name," the rat says, "Also did you name after some sort of bar codeword?"

"No…" Rein lies.

"Bartender! Why are you talking to that disgusting thing!"

Dr. Fully shots at him.

"Well…it's because they are my…pet!" Rein says. Angel

then lightly hits Rein, "Wait did you just call me, bartender?"

"Well…sorry, but I was afraid of you freaking out, and I was

planning on telling you eventually about us. So, we may or may

not have already given you a nickname," Dr. Fully admits.

"Great," Rein, now Bartender, groans.

They head downstairs again to see everyone staring at

Bartender, and the Coven Clan Rein is off the counter.

"Sorry about that. It seems are new friend is a bit scared of

the Coven Clan, but on the bright side! He's Bartender! And now

we don't have to give him id!" Dr. Fully says.

"I'm still going to steal drinks regardless," The dirty Rein

says.

"No! You guys still have to show id! *Pause* Wait, what!?!"

Bartender asks.

"Don't worry! All are scared of the Coven Clan,

however…right now I don't bite! I'm Mob by the way, nice to

meet you!" The counter Rein says as he approaches Bartender. He

reaches out his hand to shake, however Bartender pushes it aside.

"Rude," Mob replies, and steps back.

"Bartender, that Rein with causal clothing is Chicken," Dr.

Fully says.

"Because he's a scaredy cat!" Mob laughs.

"N-no I am not!" Chicken replies hastily. Mob then charges

at him, which makes Chicken flinch. He then stops and laughs on

how he's right. Dr. Fully glares at him, and he stops laughing,

and mumbles an apology, and something about he should be

moving on by now.

"I probably would summon a perdition just to make sure that one stops existing," Bartender thinks to himself about Mob. Bartender also notice that Chicken, Dr. Fully, Trash, and Cop were glaring at Mob, as well. Seems like Bartender isn't the only one with a problem with Mob.

"And that one is named, Scout," Dr. Fully says and points to the dirty Rein. Scout has his arms crossed and rolls his eyes at Dr. Fully.

"Hey, um Bartender," Trash says and grabs Bar's shoulder, "Could you get us a few drinks? I'll show you, my id!"

Bartender reluctantly agrees, and soon he's serving up drinks. All the stools at the counter are taken. He mumbles about how he wishes his other employees were with him, but serves them up with the same love and care he does at home.

Chapter 4

During this Angel whispers to him, "Hey maybe gather some evidence, by asking them some questions," Bartender agrees, and starts asking the others some questions, about who they are. He first asks Mob, who he is.

"I'm…part of the Coven Clan, and even though they are left without me in these timelines," He moves his arm to wave at the other Reins, "I'm sure they're **almost** as frightful as they are in mine. Heh," Mob says, but he then mumbles, "Keep telling yourself that Rein,"

"H-how did you join?"

"One of the members found me, and offered me to join,"

Mob says, "Hey, how about you ask Chicken something!"

Bartender goes to Chicken next, and asks him about who he

is.

"O-oh! I-I'm a scientist! L-like Dr. Fully! W-we actually

worked in the same lab in our respective timelines. Ha! I didn't

know Blatant Labs could exist in other timelines!" Chicken

replies.

"Why did you become a scientist?"

"My parents encourage me to follow my dreams and

become one!" Chicken replies happily.

"Lucky," Bartender responds. Guess not only their

profession can change, but their past as well.

Bartender then asks Dr. Fully on who he is.

"I'm Dr. Rein Fully! The inventor of the timeline hopper, and the first timeline hopper! I'm currently researching the different timelines, how they occur, and the possibility of world hopping! It's like timeline hopping, but instead of a parallel universe of your current timeline. It's an entire world! Like one wear magic is real, one where all animals are sentient, or a mix of both! And I'll be the first to find out!" Dr. Fully says. Muffled laughter is heard. Bartender tries to look for where the sound came from, but it makes him look at the strange ivy, which he now notices has two weird pods growing out on one of its stems, that looked like closed bat wings, and some mismatched thorns on one of the same stem. Bartender looks away from the creepy plant again.

"Hey! Don't laugh at me!" Dr. Fully says, and it takes a moment for Bartender to recollect his thoughts to respond.

"I didn't laugh!" Bartender pleads, "Um, how did you become a scientist?"

"Same way Chicken did!" Dr. Fully spits, "Go talk to Cop or something!"

Bartender obliges and goes to Cop, and asks him the question.

"I'm a cop…" Cop responds.

"Why?" Bartender asks.

"I-I did it because my best friend, was a cop," Cop tells him calmly, but a bit sadly as well.

"Was?"

"Oh! You know! Sometimes people default to past tense. He's still a cop! Don't worry about it," Cop answers back quickly.

"Ok…" Bartender replies. He then goes to the other sad Rein, and asks him the question he asked everybody.

"Doesn't matter go talk to someone else," Scout huffs.

"I think it does-" Bartender tries to say before being usher away, by Scout to Trash.

"Oh! You already know this. There's nothing else," Trash replies.

"Ok…why did you become a garbage man?"

"Because I needed a job? Isn't that why anyone gets an occupation?" Trash replies confusingly.

"HEY! How about you tell us about yourself, Bartender!" Mob shouts.

"Um…I'm the owner of Savior's Bar," Bartender says.

"And why???????????" Mob shouts back.

"Cause…sometimes, you have to look inside yourself, and realize that you will be homeless for the rest of your life until you do something about it. Basically, I saw an opportunity, and grabbed it. It has led me down to becoming the owner of a bar," Bartender admits.

"Inspirational!" Dr. Fully shouts.

"Wow!" Chicken replies.

"All by yourself?" Trash, Cop, and Mob say at the exact same time.

"I don't buy it," Scout sighs. He then glares at Bartender with envy, and Bartender swears the plant moved. He is staying away from the thing.

Eventually, everyone gets tired, and heads for bed.

"Wait, we are all stuck here! Where are we going?! My bar isn't a hotel!" Bartender asks when they start leaving.

"Well, this isn't your bar, and there is this door," Trash points to the strange door, on the side of the wall, which is right next to the creepy ivy, "That leads to this hallway with seven rooms," Trash responds.

"Wait! Seven rooms? How could I've not notice this! That means who ever set this up, must have intended seven people, and there are seven of us…That means we are getting dangerously close to finding out why we are here! Ooo! This is exciting! And also, very scary!" Dr. Fully shouts.

"Um, maybe God? Since maybe s-they wanted to punish us, for timeline hopping?" Bartender responds. Angel then slaps his neck again.

"Oh please! God doesn't exist! Only science!" Dr. Fully responds. He then opens the door, which does indeed show a hallway, and the rest of the Reins go into it, except Bartender.

"Hey, I think you should go into those rooms. You might catch the criminal that way," Angel whispers to Bartender.

"That's a good idea. Thanks Angel," Bartender whispers back.

"You're welcome!" Angel whispers their response.

Bartender goes into the last room, because the early bird gets the worm, and Bartender was the lazy sloth in this situation, and settles down. The room has a bed, couple of drawers, and table with a chair. The floor has huge eye carved into it, but it seems

odd though. Like someone drew a picture of an eye, and then

flipped the image in some sort of way. Somehow, it makes the eye

look companionate. Suddenly a notepad, pencil, and an orb that

glows of light appear on the table. Bartender checks it out, and

realizes this is his detective equipment.

"Nice!" Angel says and hops out of Bartender's collar. They

check the stuff out, and then runs to Bartender's bed. They hop on

top of it, and then they lay on the pillow.

"Guess, I'm sleeping without it," Bartender sighs. He

pockets the notepad and pencil, and goes to bed.

Chapter 5

Creak, slam. Pat, pat, pat, pat, pat, pat, pat, pat, pat, pat, pat, pat. Creak, slam. Bartender wakes up, after hearing this and gets up to investigate. Unfortunately, the door out of the room he is staying in is now locked from the outside, with a note on the inside of the door that reads, "Sorry, but this is supposed to be a mystery. So, you can't figure out who did it. Until more stuff happens. -Susie." Bartender rolls his eyes at this, but then he hears: *Creak, slam. Pat, pat, pat, pat, pat, pat, pat, pat, pat, pat, pat, pat, pat, pat, pat. Creak, slam.* A few minutes passes. Then *Creak, slam. Pat, pat, pat, pat.*

Creak…slam. Pat, pat, pat, pat. Creak, slam.

"I wish I knew what was going on," Bartender complains.

"Ugh, maybe it's a murder? Or something?" Angel groans

while waking up.

"If it was, there would have been a scream," Bartender

observes.

"Maybe they died before they could…" Angel says and

starts trying to get comfortable to go back to sleep.

"That's comforting," Bartender says sarcastically. After a few

more moments, the pats came back, with a *creak, slam. Pat, pat, pat,*

pat, pat, pat, pat, pat, pat, pat, pat, pat. Creak, slam. An eternity

passes.

"Can I **please** leave my room!" Bartender groans, and slams

his fists on the door. Suddenly, *Creak, slam. Pat, pat, pat, pat, pat,*

pat, pat, pat.

"Are you ok in there?!" called one of the Reins, who appears to be just outside of Bartender's room. Unfortunately, Bartender doesn't know the Reins well enough to distinguish them from each other, so he's in the dark.

"No…" Bartender answers.

"Don't answer! He might be the murderer!" Angel aggressively whispers.

"What is with you and murder!" Bartender aggressively whispers back at them. Suddenly another set of pats are heard. *Creak, slam. pat, pat, pat, pat, pat, pat.* "Wait! Mob don't!" The Rein outside Bartender's door pleads. *Pat, pat, pat, pat, pat, pat, pat, pat, pat, pat, pat, pat, pat, pat, pat, pat, pat, pat. SLAM!* Mob's pats were aggressive, so when the slam was heard it isn't too surprising that something bad happened.

"G-Get off!" The Rein outside of Bartender's door shouts, "I didn't do anything!"

"Then why did you run around dragging stuff!" Mob shouts.

"We got our murderer!" Angel responds in delight.

"Shush!" Bartender responds. A bunch of other pats are heard. Bartender couldn't distinguish them, because more than one person is making them.

"Get off of him!" A Rein shouts. Bartender tries to open the door once again, and this time it works. He sees Trash on the floor in the corner. Cop is currently holding Mob down, while Dr. Fully watches. Bartender looks at the scene and asks, "How did this happen?"

"You…help…wanted…" Trash tries to speak but soon goes unconscious.

"I kept hearing infuriating sounds while I was asleep! I had enough, and I found the culprit!" Mob says but it is muffled a bit.

"Ugh…well I think it was you who made the noises. Probably snooping around where you shouldn't," Cop tells him.

"Wait where's Chicken and Scout?" Dr. Fully asks. The door on Bartender's right opens. It's Scout.

"I'm here…" Scout complains. He then slams the door shut and goes back to sleep.

"Ok, now where's Chicken!" Dr. Fully exclaims. Nobody says anything.

"Oh dear! I think the commotion scared him. Poor thing," Dr. Fully says. He then runs down the hallway to the third door from the door out. He opens it and goes inside. After a few moments, Dr. Fully runs out and shouts, "HE'S GONE! WHO TOUCHED MY CHILD!" He runs back to the group, and kicks Mob in the face, "I should've known we couldn't have trusted you! But I was so fascinated to learn about the Coven Clan so I can prevent another 'Body of Coven' Unfortunately, you are no better than them! Now tell me what did you do to my brother!"

Dr. Fully monologues with cruelty. Mob looks as hurt on the

inside as he is on the outside, but Bartender's mind pauses on

'Body of Coven'.

It seems as if the attack caused by Coven Clan towards

Blatant Labs had happened in the other timelines. Bartender

starts looking at the other Reins. Cop looks like he's going to

burst into tears, but is holding on. Trash fell unconscious, so

Bartender didn't know how he felt about the attack, same goes

with Scout since he is trying to go back to sleep. It is at this point,

Bartender realized he has to be the voice of reason.

"Hey! We don't know if Mob did anything, and jumping to

conclusions will only make it worse. What happened to scientific

reasoning?" Bartender tells the enrage scientist.

"…You're right," Dr. Fully responds, but then looks back at

Mob, "But I have my eye on you! Cop, get off of him," Cop

hesitates but then obliges. Mob gets up, and then looks at Bartender.

"Bartender, can you get me a drink?" Mob asks soberly.

"…Sure," Bartender agrees.

"Thanks," Mob replies soberly. He then limps down the hallway. Angel jumps off the bed, and runs up to Bartender. They start climbing up him, and rest on his shoulder. Bartender doesn't mind this.

"Hey, Cop?" Dr. Fully asks.

"Yeah?" Cop replies.

"Could you carry Trash to his room?" Dr. Fully responds.

"…ok" Cop answers. He picks up Trash and carries him to the room right of Scout's. Bartender and Dr. Fully then go into the bar, but somethings off. The room seems to have changed from what they left it as. The counter is still there with 5 stools in front of it, and there are 5 tables each with 4 stools with each of them, which is the exact same number of tables that Bartender has at his actual bar. The ivy makes Bartender jump a bit, but he doesn't know why.

Before Bartender and Dr. Fully go their separate ways, Bartender asks him, "Hey, did the 'Body of Coven' happened in all the timelines?"

"No, there's an infinite number of timelines. It's possible that a Coven Clan never even existed in some. However, all the Reins that are here all experienced it in their timelines. Either by being there," Dr. Fully shot Mob a glance, "Or by word of mouth like you. I'm sorry I have to cut this conversation short. I need to look for Chicken," Bartender nods, and watches Dr. Fully leave.

Chapter 6

Mob is already sitting on a stool and waiting for Bartender to come up. Bartender goes to the back bar area, and starts making Mob a drink. During this, he starts interrogating Mob.

"So, you were awoken by foot walking?"

"I didn't do it,"

"Ok, but I need information to clear your name. So, what did you do when you first woke up?"

"…I tried going back to sleep,"

"Uh, huh,"

"I heard something being dragged across the floor. Then I heard walking again, and I felt something was wrong because of the dragging. I wanted to stop whoever it was, and silence the person who was walking so I could go back to sleep, so I went outside of my room, and attacked," Mob says.

"Who was the person you attacked?" Bartender asks.

"TRASH! You were behind the door!" Mob shouts.

"Hm. What's your relationship with Chicken?" Bartender asks.

"…we are nothing," Mob answers.

"Are you sure? I'm pretty sure, Chicken was affected by the Coven Clan, since he works at Blatant Labs,"

"He…does work there,"

"But Dr. Fully works at Blatant Labs as well, and he's not Chicken. So, something happened to him to make him different from Dr. Fully,"

"Where are you going with this?"

"Well, Chicken says he became a scientist because of his parents' encouragement. Something…I didn't have,"

"Welcome to the club. Those two are the only lucky ones,"

"Yes, but it seems strange that they ended up the exact same job, but why is Chicken different?"

"It's because he's built differently,"

"No. We are all still the same person. We may act a little different, but in the end, we are all of the same blood. I think," Bartender didn't want to say this, because implies someone he respects doing something cowardly, "Something happened to Chicken, during the attack, which traumatized him deeply. I think Ni- a police officer who saved the day didn't sacrifice himself in his timeline"

"…that's the one difference between him and Dr. Fully,"

"?"

"He's not scared, because of some random fear sticking out. It's because it traumatized him,"

"!"

"He almost died during the attack, and because of this he wouldn't look me in the eye. I knew Dr. Fully was sheltering him from me, but I didn't know he wanted to use me," Mob slams his fist on the counter. Bartender almost shouted at him for doing that, and that he only has the one counter, until he remembers this isn't his bar.

"I think that's why he automatically blamed me, because I'm a part of the Clan that almost killed Chicken. I mean I WOULD BLAM THE CLAN THAT ALMOST DESTROYED MY LIVELY HOOD AND TRAMATISED SOMEONE I CONSIDERED A BROTHER! I joined the clan, so I can have a family, but I don't know if I can handle messing peoples' lives up! Scout does it so

easily. If you want my opinion…he's the one who messed with Chicken…tonight,"

"One last thing…If you wanted anything in the world. What would it be?"

"…A better life than what I have. I don't know if I can continue stealing for our leader's revenge, and doing the weird witchcraftey stuff anymore…."

"GUYS! I FOUND BLOOD!" Dr. Fully interrupts. Everyone runs up to him, except Scout, Trash, and Cop who are somewhere else. They look down and see a small drop of blood. It's near the stools, but far enough away that whoever's bleed didn't do it near the counter.

"It looks fresh, but it could be a scrap," Bartender adds.

"Or the murderer cleaned it up!" Angel whispers. Dr. Fully looks up at Bartender and sees Angel.

"Gah! Why do you have that pest as a pet!" Dr. Fully says.

"Looks like someone didn't have to sleep in a cardboard box with rats," Mob giggles. Bartender smiles at this.

"Please don't tell me you ran away from your home like Mob did too!" Dr. Fully tells Bartender.

"Honestly I'm more surprised that you had good parents," Bartender responds.

"Ugh! Why are you two and Scout the only stupid ones! Anyways, I think, Chicken might be in trouble. You see, there is someone in the kitchen…" Dr. Fully says, going back on topic.

"What?!" Bartender and Mob speaks at the exact same time.

"Look for yourself!" Dr. Fully responds. The three Reins go to the kitchen door, and try to open it but it's locked. Muffled struggling is heard. Strange…the voice of who it belongs to seems familiar. Unfortunately, Bartender can't pin-point who it is.

"Don't worry! We'll get you out of their eventually!" Dr. Fully shouts at the door, which freaks out the person behind the door more. Dr. Fully then turns to the others, "Hm. Maybe the

ever-changing locks will help with this. We just need to wait until

the phenomenon that causes the doors that don't have locks to

lock, and vice versa to happen to this door." Everyone hears

unexplained laughter.

"HEY!" Dr. Fully shouts, "Stop laughing at me!"

"Hey we aren't laughing!" Mob defends.

"Hmf! I'm going to check the attic for Chicken be right

back," Dr. Fully says and leaves in a huff.

"Hey…guys" Trash says this as he appears out of nowhere.

"Gah! What are you doing here?!" Mob gasps.

"Just hanging out?" Trash asks.

"Oh sure! Like some guilty party just causally trying to hide

evidence!" Mob says.

"Calm down! I didn't do anything!"

"Yeah, calm down Mob, we don't know if Trash is guilty or not. If I'm giving you a chance, you're going to give Trash a chance!" Bartender says.

"…Fine, I'm…sorry Trash. Wait, why don't you hold anything against me?" Mob asks.

"Um…thanks I guess…" Trash says, "The reason why I'm not angry about it is because I have this friend that showed me that you shouldn't focus on the past, and to always keep going. Actually, he inspired me to get a job, heh," Trash says.

"Oh! Same! I was down on my luck, and someone I actually came and helped me. She actually got me into the Coven Clan! Maybe we aren't so different after all!" Mob says excitedly.

"Oh…uh don't get your hopes up…hehe," Trash responds. Even the most forgiving of the Reins doesn't trust Mob.

"Hey…Trash. Could I ask you some questions?" Bartender asks.

"Sure, I guess?" Trash responds.

"What were you doing at the time before you got out of bed?" Bartender asks.

"Sleeping? Like I'm supposed to?"

"Did you hear anything?"

"Only you banging on the door…OH! I did hear some Reins leave their rooms! It was a little loud though…I think it was someone next to me? I don't know I was busy sleeping,".

"Hm…what's your relationship with Chicken?"

"Oh! We are really good friends! Not as much as him and Dr. Fully. Speaking of Dr. Fully, where is he? I know he went to check on the attic, but shouldn't he have come down by now?" This reasoning is enough to get the three Reins moving towards the stairs, and up to the attic. While they are moving, Bartender ask Trash a final question, "If you could get anything you ever wanted, what would it be?"

"Oh! That's easy! The friend that helped me through that rough time that I had, lost his arm recently…So, I would ask to heal him! You know…to pay him back for what he did," Trash says honestly.

"Is your friend a cop?" Bartender asks.

"Oh definitely! Why do you ask?" Trash answers.

"No-Actually I have a fri-regular that is a cop, and he has lost his arm recently as well. Is your friend's name Niko Huva?" Bartender asks. He is a bit hesitant to explain himself, and he isn't going to admit Niko and him are friends. Right now, he didn't even want to admit to himself that he considers Niko as his friend. It's not because he doesn't want friends, it's just Bartender believes he doesn't deserve any.

"YES! I didn't realize he's the bar loving type!" Trash says.

"Ugh! I don't care about a stupid po-po person let's just seEEEEEEEE!" Mob interrupts himself at the sight.

Dr. Fully is white pale and unconscious due to fainting. The sight in front of him reveals why he fainted in the first place. Trash, and Bartender gag at the sight of Chicken's remains, who is now on the floor with a big fat hole in his head.

Bartender feels tears going down his face. He didn't know Chicken for long, but losing a life is something tragic. It also gives him the uncomfortable thought about if Niko died in the attack, Bartender would most likely not morn him at all.

"I'm…so…sorry, Chicken," Trash says looking like he's about to faint.

"Oh…my… gosh," Bartender says while feeling dizzy. Fortunately, Angel is there to slap him out of it.

"Oh. Oh, no," Mob says and runs to Chicken. He checks the body before saying in a shocked, scared tone, "H-he's dead…" A moment of silence is heard.

Chapter 7

"I told you!" Angel whispers to Bartender. Bartender gently smacks Angel on the head.

"Don't boo me! I'm right!" Angel aggressively whispers back.

"Let's get…Dr. Fully out of here," Trash says in almost a whisper. The three Reins pick up the fallen Rein and drag him back downstairs, where Cop and Scout are waiting. They seem to be in a bad mood, as per usual.

"Hey, what do you got there?" Scout says.

"Dr. Fully. He fainted," Trash says. They lie him down on the floor, and Bartender runs off and brings back some alcohol. He pours it down on Dr. Fully's face.

"Ok, what happened?" Cop asks.

"C-chickens d-dead," Trash forcefully musters out. Scout and Cop give a shocked expression, but it's a bit delayed. Dr. Fully starts waking up.

"*Cough* Why are you pouring alcohol on my face?" Dr. Fully says angrily, and sits up, but then his memories come rushing back, and he breaks out in a sob.

"Why? Didn't he suffer enough? Why must he be taken from us…me? Why!" Dr. Fully sobs, "I **will** find the culprit! Chicken for you! Cop! Go search around the attic! No wait stay here…you're a suspect. Everyone stay here since you are all known suspects. I will go and search for evidence! Bartender, could you please serve us up some drinks? I think I need one…"

"Ok," Bartender responds, as the poor doctor runs off to search for clues. Bartender looks at the others. They all seem so sad, except Scout, who appears to not care. Bartender now realizes this is what Mob meant on how Scout is the most likely suspect. However, that's too obvious. Bartender goes to the back bar, and sighs.

"I wish Selvester was here…He would've been able to help take the orders, while I can investigate," Bartender accidently says out loud. Even though Bartender automatically assumes he can do this by himself, he didn't realize how much he relied on Selvester. Especially after seeing that murder, Bartender wished he had someone like Niko or Selvester to comfort him.

"Wait, Selvester? As in Selvester Twity?" Trash asks.

"Yeah, what about him?" Bartender says, realizing his mistake.

"He's so sweet, and always tips! Heh. I'm sure he wouldn't want to spend time with a person like me though. His brother, Richard is cool too! He's my best friend's partner! I sometimes get jealous on how much he spends time with Niko. I'm not gay though! Ha-ha! Just wish I could spend more time with him that's all!" Trash monologues.

"You're right you aren't gay. You're pan," Cop says.

"What! No! Just straight! Even if I know what pan means anyways ha-ha!" Trash says in a rush manner. He's blushing.

"YOU ARE PAN LIKE THE REST OF US, TRASH!" Mob shouts at him, "ACCEPT IT!"

"Dude. Even **I** know I'm pan, what's your excuse?" Scout says.

"I…I AM STRAIGHT AS A LINE!" Trash shouts, while blushing.

"Sssssssure. Whatever helps you sleep at night," Bartender

says. Angel chuckles.

"UGH! USELESS! I'M LEAVING!" Trash shouts in huff. He

then goes to the door that leads to the hallway.

"Huh. Selvester had a brother. I never knew that, but I mean,

maybe that's why he's always so sad all the time. Maybe

something happened to him," Scout says.

"Wow! You can focus on someone other than yourself!?"

Mob says sarcastically.

"Takes one, to know one," Scout replies. Mob huffs at this.

"Wait, what's your relationship with him?" Bartender asks

Scout.

"Eh. He sometimes comes by the check if I'm alright, but I

know it's just volunteer work. Nothing to it," Scout says.

"Volunteer work?" Bartender asks him.

"None of your business," Scout says.

"Murderer…" Mob hisses.

"We don't know that yet," Bartender corrects him.

"Honestly, if you are really sure Scout might not be the killer then you should ask more people about what happened. Like Cop," Mob tells Bartender.

"Good idea. Hey, Cop! Can I ask you a few questions?" Bartender asks Cop.

"Um…sure?" Cop says.

"Do you know a man named Richard?" Bartender asks him.

"Um…who?" Cop asks.

"Well, you're a cop, right?"

"Yes, Captain Obvious,"

"Do you know who Niko is?"

"Of course! He's my partner, and…my best friend," Cop says this somberly, but flusters a little at "my best friend".

"Is Niko the one who convinced you to join the police force?"

"Yeah…"

"Richard is Niko's partner, so it makes sense if you actually met him before,"

"NO! Richard is **not** Niko's partner! **I am**!"

"The facts say otherwise," Bartender says.

"Can confirm! I've seen a person that looks similar to Selvester next to a cop. It would make sense if that look-a-like is Richard. Huh, that means Richard is partners with a coward," Mob confirms this, but it's Mob so nobody cares, especially when Bartender and Cop are irritated by Mob calling Niko that.

"No, they don't," Scout objects.

"Ok…why?" Bartender says.

"If I could remember correctly…Richard is dead in my timeline," Scout says, "I think when he was…uh 12-14? A possible reason Cop never met Richard is because Richard died

before becoming a cop."

"Yeah…that's right!" Cop says.

"You just got owned," Angel whispers to Bartender. He hits

them playfully in response. Bartender ponders this new evidence.

If Richard is dead in Scout's timeline, then it would make sense

that Scout's Selvester is sad. Bartender only met Richard a couple

of times, usually he was with Niko, but Bartender could only

imagine what Selvester is/was going through because of it.

Bartender remembers what Richard looks like however. He has

sliver eyes like his brother, but his hair was much darker. His face

structure was almost exactly the same as Selvester's, but Richard

just like Niko, is missing an arm. Unlike Niko though, he has a

prospect arm to compensate, and isn't planning on turning the

hand into a gun. Perhaps that missing arm was caused by

whatever incident that caused Scout's Richard to die.

Bartender's pondering is interrupted by Trash running in with a stool. Everyone, including Dr. Fully, stops whatever they are doing to see. Everyone comes over and sees the stool in all of its glory. It's the murder weapon.

Chapter 8

The seat is covered in a fatal amount of blood. Some of the Reins gag a little.

"I was searching through some of our rooms to see any evidence for," Trash interrupts his speech and looks up in the attic, but then goes back to it, "w-what happened, and I found this in Mob's room…I think we all know who did it now," Trash says. Everyone looks at Mob.

"I DID'T DO IT! Someone must have tried to frame me! Who hates me enough to do that!" Mob says in a panic.

"Mob…I'm the only person in this room who doesn't hate your guts," Scout responds, "Guess everyone is a suspect,"

"T-then it's Dr. Fully! I'm the first one to the door, and he's right next to me! He probably killed Chicken then went to my room to hide the murder weapon!" Mob pleads.

"HOW DARE YOU ACCUSE ME OF MURDERING CHICKEN!" Dr. Fully shouts, "GET HIM DOWN!" All the Reins, except Bartender and Scout run up to Mob. Mob tries fighting back but it's useless. He gives up.

"Where shall we take him?" Trash asks.

"To the attic! So, he can see what he has done!" Cop spits.

"Wait! Guys! I think we are doing this all wrong! He might be still innocent!" Bartender pleads.

"Then why didn't he see the murder weapon?" Trash responds, "It was in his room!"

Bartender didn't have an answer for him, yet. So, he watches helplessly as the Reins drag Mob up the stairs while he shouts, "IT ISN'T ME!" Over and over, and over. Eventually they come back down, without Mob. A moment of silence passes. The worst part of it is, Bartender doesn't actually know Mob is innocent, so this could be justice. However, something in his gut is telling him that Mob is innocent.

"So, what now?" Trash asks.

"I'm going to get rid of his timeline hopper," Dr. Fully says in upset voice.

"That seems too easy on him," Cop says.

"Are you saying we kill him?" Scout says.

"*Pause* No. I just think taking away his weekend plans at Bartender's bar or hanging out with that other timeline's chick is not going to be a great enough punishment," Cop responds.

"Another timeline's chick?" Bartender asks.

"We don't just visit each other's and your timeline, with the timeline hopper," Dr. Fully says, "You're just the common factor that we all went to. Wait a minute…" Dr. Fully starts quietly monologuing to himself about this new discovery.

"Anyways, I think we are still hopping to this answer too quickly. I think we should give him a fair trial," Bartender tells the others.

"…Tomorrow. After, I…we recover," Dr. Fully says.

"Is Mob trapped there?" Angel asks the scientist, but hides it as though Bartender said it.

"No. As the luck would have it, the door locked, and Trash just so happened to receive a key in his pocket," Dr. Fully shows a key in his hands, "I don't know where it came from, but I am going to hold on to it. Until everything works out," Dr. Fully says. His eyes water. Surprisingly, Cop runs over and hugs him.

"Cop?" Dr. Fully says.

"I'm sorry for your loss. Believe me, it's hard," Cop responds.

"I…believe you. You know better than anyone," Dr. Fully responds, and hugs him.

"Don't worry, we'll get justice for his death," Cop responds. They stop hugging and Dr. Fully says, "Rest up! I'm going to interrogate Mob. We need the rest to…properly take care of Mob," Dr. Fully then goes upstairs. The others head back to their rooms. Bartender notices Scout whispering to himself.

"What are you whispering?" Bartender asks.

"I'm counting…" Scout responds.

"Why?" Bartender asks.

"UGH! When we were all sleeping, some Reins got out of their rooms and walked about. I'm counting my steps, so if it happens again…I will know who did it,"

"So…how many steps between the doors?"

"None of your business," Scout says, and runs off to his

room.

Chapter 9

Because of Scout's counting, Bartender decides to find out where all Reins are staying, and how far are they from the door. He goes into his room and writes down all he knows, and the memory of where each Rein, he believes is staying.

He's the farthest away from the door, and next is Scout's room. He couldn't forget that downer. Dr. Fully is right next to Mob, and Mob himself is directly next to the door. It's because he heard dragging in the bar, and nobody else spoke up about it.

Bartender realizes that he should go ask Mob for more information about it.

He gets up and walks to the attic. He sees the door is still locked, with Mob still inside.

"Mob?" Bartender asks.

"Who is it? We all have the same voice," says a very somber sounding person.

"Bartender. Are you doing alright?" Bartender asks.

"I'm trapped in the same room as a rotting corpse, while everyone thinks I killed him. I'm doing great!" Mob says sarcastically.

"Ok…I want to talk to you about that **dragging** you heard,"

"I don't know what it was. It's probably Scout dragging the body up into the attic,"

"We don't know if it's Scout or not, so just say murderer," Bartender corrects him.

"Hmf! But actually now that I think about it, the dragging didn't sound like someone dragging a body up the stairs. It felt like someone was dragging a body across the floor to the right, but either way there was a door that opened,"

"Could this 'body' be the mysterious person in the kitchen?"

"If that's the case, then I'm useless," Mob says. Bartender realizes that Mob was most likely asleep during the murder.

"Why didn't you see the murder weapon?"

"Rage,"

"Did you see anyone go into your room?"

"…No. I was asleep,"

That conforms it, or Mob's just lying. Maybe hoping Mob is innocent is just a big mistake.

As if Mob read Bartender's mind, he replies "It wasn't me! I know I sound suspicious, but it wasn't me! If it was me, I would have used one of my trusty daggers that I always have on me!"

Bartender hears scratching on the door. Demonstration, perhaps. However, that's not going to be enough…there has to be a way to prove he didn't do it, or get him to confess. Then Bartender remembers the steps.

"Wait. I woke up earlier than you. So, I heard some steps. I don't remember the exact number of pats," Bartender chuckles to himself, "But I did remember a shorter walk, and then an opening of a door. However, this door closed later than the other doors. Since you are the closest to the door to the bar, it's a good chance that, that walk might have been to your room, and the pause was someone framing you!"

"YES! Finally! Evidence that proves I'm innocent! MATH!" Trash then comes up from behind Bartender.

"Excuse me, Bar," Trash tells him, "Could I speak with the killer? I need to know why he did it." Bartender reluctantly obliges, but before Bartender goes down the flight of stairs to leave Trash and Mob alone. He asks Trash, "Where are you staying at?"

"Me? Oh! I'm staying at the 5th door from the bar," Trash tells him. Bartender thanks him, and goes down the stairs. As soon as Bartender reaches the door to the hallway, he hears Trash shout, "HOW DARE YOU CLAIM YOU ARE INNOCENT! COVEN CLAN CAUSED MY NIKO TO LOSE HIS ARM! YOU ARE AN UNJUSTLY INDIVIDUAL! STOP PRETENDING YOU ARE NOT!" Bartender is now glad he left the two of them alone. He goes back to his room, and writes down where Trash was. He then decides to do the obvious, and count his steps. There are 4 pats between each door. Bartender takes note of this.

Before Bartender could exit the hallway and go into the bar, he sees Trash walk past him angerly. Most likely from the argument he had. Trash storms off to the fifth door away from the hallway's exit door. He opens it, goes inside, and slams it shut.

Seems this confirms he didn't lie about it. Bartender enters the bar and sees Dr. Fully moving stools, and tables around.

"What are you doing?" Bartender asks him.

"Preparing for the trial!" Dr. Fully answers, "Wanna help?"

"Sure," Bartender replies, and the two start working on the trial set-up together.

"Mind if I ask you a few questions?" Bartender says.

"Only if you allow me to ask you some," Dr. Fully answers. Dr. Fully starts asking Bartender questions on what he did during the time period, and Bartender answers them truthfully.

"Huh, that explains why Trash was right next to your room," Dr. Fully answers.

"Trash is my witness," Bartender says.

"I'm glad you wanted to help. It's a shame the door locked from the outside," Dr. Fully says.

"Yeah, what were you doing at that time?"

"I was unfortunately sleeping. *Sigh* If I'd known…"

"It's ok-"

"No. I'm alright! I'll… tell his family what happened to

him,"

Even though he already knew where Dr. Fully's room was

he decides to ask him anyways.

"Right next to Chicken's!" Dr. Fully answers, and before

Bartender can tell him to be more specific Dr. Fully interrupts by

saying, "I think you should be the defense,"

"Um…I'm not attorney, and besides I feel like I would

definitely mess it up…" Dr. Fully runs up to him, and places his

hands on Bartender's shoulders. This causes Angel to jump off.

"1. None of us are, but we are still doing it anyways, and 2.

more importantly, we are both of the same blood. I became the

first scientist that has ever timeline hopped, and you became a

successful business owner, with the best bar in the multiverse. We both achieved great things, and we are both the same person! I

believe you can do this. Besides, you are the only person that

wanted to see justice by looking at facts instead of rushing it in

like we all did!"

"…I…really don't deserve your praise, Dr. Fully," Bartender

grabs Dr. Fully's hands. He sets the hands down, and then lets

them go. Suddenly, Angel runs off and goes behind the counter.

Both Reins turn to look at them.

"Troublesome rat!" Dr. Fully spits, "I bet it is trying to get

into this bar's liquor."

"Or…they have some common sense," says a very sinister

voice behind the two Reins. They both turn to see who it is.

Chapter 10

The ivy is no longer there, but in its place is a 7ft perdition.

He has brown hair, and lime green eyes. His horns are leafy green

colored, but mismatched in size. His wings are bat wings, which

is colored leafy green, with the skin part being lime. For some

reason, the perdition wears lip stick, which is dark purple, but

almost seems like it's black. His clothes looked like they were

made of the plant ivy. He flicks his leathery tail, which has a

lemon shape tip, with two holes that make the end of his tail look

like an eye. He is in a pose like a stereotypical popular mean girl.

Bartender couldn't tell what gender he is. Dr. Fully babbles at the sheer impossibility of it.

"But…demons…angels…gods…aren't…real!" Dr. Fully stampers out.

"There is a lot of things that are real," the perdition answers.

"W-Who are you?" Bartender asks, trying to sound as brave as he could.

"My name is Envicha. An Envy Perdition," the perdition answers. Dr. Fully starts trying to quietly make his way towards the hallway door.

"W-what do you want?" Bartender asks, while feeling an unexplained feeling of dread.

"Anything you have really, but right now: your eternal screams for my collection," Envicha tells Bartender. Then he turns into a lion (keeping with wings, horns, and tail) and pounces. Bartender tries fighting the creature off, but Envicha quickly overpowers the Rein. Dr. Fully runs towards the door. Suddenly, the perdition stops what they were doing to Bartender, turns into a stork, (with his horns, and wings, and the added bonus of tail feathers having the eye symbol on it. All that jazz), and flies towards Dr. Fully. Bartender quickly gets to his feet, and leaps for Envicha's feet. He grabs hold of the perdition's feet and tries to slow the perdition down. It doesn't do much, but it allows Dr. Fully to run into the hallway.

Suddenly the door to the hallway disappears, and is quickly replaced by the exact same door, but with the eye the perdition has on his tail, but flipped. Envicha kicks Bartender off of his feet, which causes the bar owner to fall to the ground, and he turns back to a human. He slams his fists against the door, and then turns towards Bartender and growls, "…**you**," Bartender instinctively gets up and starts backing away. The perdition turns into a lion, and charges at Bartender. Bartender barely manages to dodge, which again ends up with him on the floor. Envicha slams into some of the tables, but recovers quickly. The perdition then turns into a big snake, and once again charges at Bartender. This time, he catches him, and coils the Rein up. Bartender tires to break free but fails.

"You know," Envicha says while still in the snake form, "I was going to knock you unconscious and frame you for the murder. However, I guess framing someone else for two murders might be more **satisfying**," Before Bartender can call for help, he feels his breathe being forced out of him, as now he's being squeezed to death. He coughs trying again to speak, when suddenly he is no longer being squeezed, but he still can't breathe. It's because there is no oxygen outside of the bar. Bartender can see the bar's exterior, which makes the bar look like the outside of a video game's map.

"Sorry! I forgot!" Susie says, and Bartender realizes that she is right next to him. Suddenly, a bubble forms around Bartender, giving him oxygen and other stuff a human needs to survive in space, or where ever Bartender is.

"You…saved me," Bartender tells her, while catching his breathe.

"I know! I just couldn't let my contr-detective die!" Susie says, "Good thing you dodge that lion attack…It's easier to put things in and out of existence than teleportation!"

"What now?" Bartender asks her.

"We wait until it finishes what it needs to do, and then I'll send you back there,"

"No thanks! That place has a demon there!"

"It's fine! That envy perdition will probably have to turn back to a plant or become docile at some point…"

"Ok, I'll bite. Why is Envicha called an Envy perdition, and does it relate to the seven deadly sins?"

"Yep! It does go back to the seven deadly sins! Each perdition has its own sin related to it, and also has the opposite savior, basically your 'Angels'. Anyways, only seven perdition and seven saviors can exist at one timeline. The goal of a perdition is to try to trick people into making deals with them, so they can get your soul, in very subtle ways. Honestly, the Wrath Perdition at one point tried to advertise to you. However, you were too stu- I mean, you weren't observing it correctly to notice. Back to the point, when deals are made most of the time the perdition is very loyal to the deal maker, and each perdition has their own way of accomplishing it. OH! Also, each type perdition can only do deals that are related to its own sin. This perdition that you are fighting against, has powers related to envy, as it told you because, it is an envy perdition. So, basically anything that deals with the envy sin, it can accomplish. This is why it is called an Envy Perdition,"

"…You really enjoy monologuing…"

"Yeah, it's a problem…" While the two waits for Envicha to finish, they talk about stuff with the range of the weather to when will the world end.

Chapter 11

"…and you see if Dr. Fully does successfully world hop, he won't be the first. That privilege goes to this annoying human-dragon thing named Melody Scales," Susie says to Bartender.

"So that's why Envicha laughed when he said he would be the first," Bartender says.

"No, that was actually me. Anyways! I think the envy perdition went back to being a plant, so it's safe to come back,"

"…I don't know. He looks like he was out for blood,"

"Hm, I'll be right back," After a second, she has a necklace, with a white circle on it, which has the flipped eye in the center, in her hand, she teleports it right on to Bartender.

"How's this supposed to help?" Bartender asks confused.

"It's a Kindness Savior's necklace. It makes the wearer immune to all of the Envy Perdition's affects. That thing won't be able to land a finger on you, if and ONLY if you wear it,"

"Ok, thank you!"

"Also! You are doing great! You actually attracted some…unwanted attention. *Sigh* My sister such a jerk. I kicked her out of course! But I just wanted to say that before I send you off, keep up the good work and good luck!"

Bartender smiles at this and suddenly he is no longer in a bubble but on the floor of the bar. He sees all the Reins talking amongst themselves, except one. Bartender looks over to them, and before he speaks up, when suddenly...

"Bartender?!" The voice came from behind the floor Rein. Bartender turns around and sees Angel looking flabbergasted, shocked, and is that joy?

"Y-yeah?" Bartender says. The yellow rat runs up to him, and jumps right on top of him.

"I-I thought you died!" Angel says holding tightly on Bartender's clothes.

"Well, I didn't! I don't understand why you care so much…" Bartender says.

"YOU MORON! OF COURSE, I WOULD CARE! YOU ARE THE ONLY FRIEND I HAVE, WHICH ADMITLY ISN'T SAYING MUCH SINCE I WAS LITERALY BORN YESTERDAY!" Angel shouts at Bartender. The Rein blushes. Friend? That can't be right…right? No one ever cared about Bartender before. It was something Bartender accepted as being a true facet of this world. He would always be alone. Is Bartender hearing this right?

"You're joking…right?" Bartender asks. Angel delivers him a slap, that tells Bartender, no.

"Bartender?" One of the Reins says. Apparently, Angel's shouting got the other's attention. Hopefully, they won't realize Angel talks. Why was he hiding that again? Eh, it's probably because Angel doesn't want to be known.

"Y-yeah?"

Dr. Fully starts running towards him, "You disappeared! I thought that you might have gotten killed or something!" Bartender receives a hug from the scientist, "Wait, what is that thing on your chest?"

"It's…a necklace," Bartender says.

"Wait, where did you get that?" Cop says coming closer. He's eyeing it suspiciously.

"Well… I was temporarily teleported…uh…home! And I got this necklace for…good luck!" Bartender lies.

"Good luck? I would say superstitions are false, but that **plant** turned into a demon that attacked us, so ANYTHING goes!" Dr. Fully says, and he sounds like he's having an existential crisis. The others come closer, and help Bartender back on his feet.

"Ok, what did I miss?" Bartender says.

"Dr. Fully went insane," Scout says.

"I can see that," Bartender says.

"I AM SPEAKING THE TRUTH!" Dr. Fully says.

"Honestly, saying that plant is a demon is the **last** thing you would say," Cop says.

"HOW MANY TIMES DO I HAVE TO SAY, IF IT'S NOT SOMETHING I WOULD SAY, THEN IT IS **TRUE!!!!!**" Dr. Fully shouts.

"Besides that, we were about to go check up on Mob. Whatever happened, I'm kind of worried about him. Even if he's a filthy murderer," Trash says. The group of Reins then go upstairs, and are greeted to a door that is wide open.

"He escaped…" Scout says.

"That proves that he is guilty. Only a guilty party tries to…to" Trash says and looks inside the room.

Chicken is no longer the only corpse in the attic, and the one who seemed to have suffered the least. Angel and Trash throw up, and Dr. Fully faints yet again with Bartender. Even Scout looks like he wants to puke. Everyone decides to go back downstairs.

"…Ok, maybe Mob wasn't the murder," Trash says.

"Maybe!?" Scout shouts.

"Or there are two murderers, Trash," Cop replies.

"What do you mean?" Trash says.

"Well, we all hated Mob, and he did kill Chicken. So, what if one of us decided that we wanted revenge. Dr. Fully and Trash are now prime suspects. Especially Trash. Since he did get into a

pretty heated argument with Mob, before what happened," Cop

says.

"I didn't do it! I was pretty upset! But not enough to

murder!"

"Likely story,"

"Guys calm down! We aren't going to jump to conclusions!

Remember how Mob died!" Bartender tries to defend.

"But Mob did **kill** Chicken!" Trash says.

"With what evidence!" Bartender says.

"The stool, in his room?" Scout says sarcastically, "Or does

your tiny brain not able to comprehend what happened?"

"I..." Bartender says.

"Then we should put Trash in the attic! Now, Dr. Fully

please hand me the key so I can lock Trash up!" Cop says.

"Of course!" Dr. Fully says. He then searches his pockets, "Um, where's the key?" Scout then bumps into Bartender, then Cop, and then Trash.

"Found it, in Trash's pocket," Scout says, and reveals a key.

"Wait I didn't do it!" Trash says, "I just found it on the floor, and was going to give it back to Dr. Fully!"

"Well, he did run into the hallway. So, he could have dropped it then, but when he got it, well that's a different story" Cop says.

"Ok, what happened in the time period I was gone? I think this is something I should know," Bartender says.

"We all got locked into our rooms, I went into your room to hide from that thing, and told the others to do the same. We all heard a crash, so we all, except me of course, scrambled into the rooms. I don't know who went where, so I don't know who did it," Dr. Fully says.

"I was in my room, trying to fix my anger," Trash says.

"And I went back to my room," Cop says.

"I went back to my room as well, but there was a person who left Chicken's room," Scout says. Everybody looks at him, "I was counting how long it took for one of us to go into each room, and the number of pats to the door could only be from Chicken's room. So, one of us is lying,"

"What about Bartender? He was in the bar," Trash says.

"My new necklace is my alibi, and the perdition that tried to kill me. Dr. Fully is also my witness," Bartender responds.

"SEE! I'm **not** crazy!" Dr. Fully says.

"Ok, so Dr. Fully isn't crazy because Bartender is a witness," Trash says not fully convinced, "What was that crash though?"

"**A perdition tried to kill me**, what do you think!?" Bartender says. Suddenly, Angel with a dagger in their mouth runs tugs on Bartender's pants leg. It seems while no one was looking, Angel grabbed a knife.

"GAH! WHY DOES THAT HELLSPAWN HAVE A KNIFE!" Dr. Fully shouts.

"I dunno," Bartender says, as he picks Angel up.

"I found it on Chicken's body. It was clearly not there before…hope it helps," Angel whispers to Bartender. Bartender examens the dagger, and sees it has blood on its blade, and it's handle has a symbol similar to the ones Mob's clothing. Bartender thinks for a moment, and realizes this dagger came from the Coven Clan, because it has a 0 wielding a 1 as a sword. A common symbol related to Coven Clan.

"Bartender did…did you see any daggers in yo-this bar?" Trash asks, and grabs the knife from Rein's hands.

"No, only alcohol and glasses in it," Bartender says.

"Then where did they get the dagger?" Trash says.

"Pardon?" Bartender says.

"Well, when we all got here, we lost all of our items, except the clothes on our backs. Cop lost his baton, and gun, and Mob lost his weapons. So, where did it come from?" Trash then takes the dagger from Bartender.

"It came from Mob. He was just able to hide daggers well," A familiar voice says. Everyone turns to the plant, who is now Envicha once again. He walks over to a now flabbergasted Trash, and steals the dagger. He then proceeds to smash it up like it was nothing. Everyone, except Bartender and Dr. Fully, who ran back into the hallway, when he appears again, looks shocked. The perdition calmly turns to them and says, "I'm Envicha, an Envy Perdition. If you have any desires that focus on the Envy sin…call me, and we'll make a deal,"

Chapter 12

"WHAT IN THE NAME OF ANTS IS THAT THING!"

Trash says.

"An envy perdition, she clearly said it. Or are they a he,"

Cop says.

"I am the person who is talking to me's gender," Envicha

says, he than shrugs, "But I'm technically genderless, anyways"

"Ok, wait, why are you here?" Cop says.

"Well, I made a deal with someone here," Envicha then looks at Bartender, "Not you. You suck, and also that necklace won't protect you forever…"

"W-why d-did you b-break *gulp* that D-dagger?" Trash says.

"Well…I'm the murderer! I'm supposed to get rid of evidence!" Envicha admits.

"WHAT! Y-you're just admitting to it!" Scout says.

"I just do what I'm told. My client asked for Mob's death, since I told him Mob killed Chicken. Believe me, I was the plant when Chicken's murder took place," Envicha says.

"Then who is your client?" Scout says with the most serious tone he has ever said in the entire time Bartender's been here. Everyone, who knew him for much longer than Bartender seems shocked at this tone, as well.

Envicha just smiles and says, "Trash,"

"NO! I never meet you before in my life!" Trash says.

"Sorry, but it's true!" Envicha says.

Bartender couldn't believe it! He now has the person who made the deal! He can go home now, and catch up on the bar. He has to admit, he's been really nervous about his bar, ever since he realizes this building wasn't his bar.

"Bartender! Have you seen a mystery story before? There's always a twist! Think about it…" Angel says. Bartender thinks about it, and realizes if Trash is really Envicha's partner he is betraying Trash. Bartender decides to call the perdition out for it.

"What! **I AM NOT THAT RODENT KNOWN AS MALRAPTURE! I WOULD NEVER BETRAY MY PARTNER FOR SOME MORE SOULS! EVEN THE GREEDIER ONES WERE DISGUSTED BY WHAT THAT STUPID LUST PERDITION DID!**" Envicha shouts at him offendedly. Bartender feels smaller, and everyone rushes away from him. Angel jumps right on top of Bar's necklace, and holds on to it like a cross.

Bartender gulps and gathers strength to say his next choice of

words.

"T-then p-prove IT!" Bartender chokes, "Y-Y-You said it y-

yourself! You always do what your client wants, uh Trash! G-

Give…Give him a command!"

Everyone looks at Trash. "Um, could you please bring…

whoever it is in the kitchen, to us?" Trash asks. Envicha pauses

for a bit. It seems as if he was looking for someone else's

approval, also in this time, Dr. Fully slowly creeps back into the

bar. After a few seconds, Envicha goes into the kitchen, and

brings out…

"Niko?" almost all the Reins say this. Except, Cop and Scout.

"Niko?!?" Cop says after being a bit delayed.

Niko is bounded, gaged, and clearly terrified. The Reins, except Scout, help him. He then screams, which honestly if Bartender was in the exact situation, he would do the same.

"HAVE I BEEN DRUGGED?! WHY AM I SEEING DOUBLE OF SOME PERSON FROM COVEN CLAN! OR QUADRUPLE!" Niko screams.

"Calm down, we are just alternate versions of the same guy!" Trash says.

"THAT MAKES PERFECT SENSE!" Niko shouts, sarcastically.

"Hey, you aren't missing an arm," Trash says.

"He ain't dead either," Scout says.

"WHY WOULD I BE MISSING AN ARM!" Niko shouts.

"Because you sacrificed it to save a bunch of people at Blatant Labs!" Trash says.

"...I didn't, but I guess yours did...I was too scared," Niko says sadly. It seems he regretted whatever his choice was. This moment of not screaming in terror didn't last long, since Niko took one look at Envicha and started screaming bloody murder, and how Envicha was the one who kidnapped the terrified police officer in the first place. The perdition sighs and quickly knocks Niko out using his tail. Everyone looks at Envicha.

"What? He was freaking out and annoying me! I have the right to knock out annoyances," Envicha says.

"Why don't you kill him?" Scout asks. Envicha doesn't answer the question, "Oh, so is Niko actually involved with your deal? So, you can't kill him because that would be violating the deal!"

"Not particularly. I'm not a pure violent creature that kills anything in my path. I'm envy not wrath. I only kill people who pose a threat, in my way, or because it was the deal in the first place" Envicha says, and then starts talking like they are advertising, "By the way… is there anything you want; But someone else claimed it first, and it's something so great you would, I don't know, sell your soul for…"

"No," Scout replies.

"So, what do we do now?" Dr. Fully says, "Chicken's murderer is dead, and I'm too scared to punish a demon…but I don't want to get in his way if Trash really is Mob's killer or well the person who got Envicha to assassinate Mob,"

"Well, we could get rid of his timeline hopper," Cop says.

"Weren't you the one who said taking away a timeline hopper wasn't a good enough punishment for murder," Scout says.

"Excuse me, he sold his soul to a permanent damnation, which in my opinion is punishment enough. I just want to make sure that this perdition isn't able to switch timelines so freely, as before…imagine the chaos of two perditions," Cop says.

"Wait…something doesn't line up," Bartender says.

"Oh?" Envicha says.

"You only deal with envy related deals. You shouldn't be able to murder Mob if the reason was to take revenge. That is more wrath than envy," Bartender says.

"REALLY? Who cares if the murderer's motive wasn't envy! I still killed him! And I made **sure** he suffered, while my client watched! Did you get that information out of that sudo-scientist Orchifly!" Envicha shouts at Bartender. Clearly if Bar didn't have the necklace on, Envicha would've killed him, deal or no deal. Bartender decides that he's going to wear the necklace until he reaches the end of his days.

"Pardon? What's an Orchifly?" Dr. Fully asks.

Envicha looks at Dr. Fully and smiles evilly. "Oh, it's just the species that creates worlds like this one. $Yio* is just the name of the one who created yours, and it just so happens that this man was working with her to figure out who made a deal with me. So, he already knew that a murder was going to happen in the first place and did nothing about it," The perdition states. Everyone looks at Bartender shocked.

Chapter 13

"In my defense, Susie forced me to do this job…and I'm not the person who would deny a request from God! And I didn't know a murder was going to happen! I just wanted to find out who made the deal with Envicha in the first place, so I could go home, and continue running my bar!" Bartender defends.

"And he didn't want the murder to happen…the first time at least, he woke up early, but he was locked in his room, and I'm assuming this…Susie was causing all those locks to appear, so Bartender is just a pawn in her game," Dr. Fully says.

"Yeah, this is just an experiment for her, to see if people like us can solve our 'demon' problems…" Bartender confess.

"Is this why we are all here! FOR AN EXPERIMENT! *Pause* I think I like her…" Dr. Fully says.

"I don't understand. Aren't you guys going to fight over that lie?" Envicha says.

"This isn't a kid's movie! We aren't falling for the liar reveal trope! I think we are all madder at Susie than Bar! Like Fully said, Bartender is a pawn in Susie's game! Bartender didn't have a choice! No one had a choice in this!" Scout says.

"Well, that plan failed…" Envicha spits, "But anyways, since you were the undercover detective…you can just say to her that Trash made a deal, and now we can all go home! Just say it to her!"

"I don't know yet…I think you are lying about who made a deal with you," Bartender says.

"Oh, here we go! This idiot has integrity!" Envicha complains.

"If you really were Trash's partner. You wouldn't have betrayed Trash, you wouldn't have paused like waiting for someone to give their approval if Trash was your partner, and you would have not been able to fulfill Trash's request of revenge if you were an envy perdition, because wrath and envy, and even though they might overlap at times, are two different things," Bartender says.

Envicha turns into a dragon. "OK! If you want to go, **there**! Tell the class! I dare you! TELL THE CLASS! WHO WAS THE ONE WHO MADE A DEAL WITH **ME**! AND IF IT'S WRONG! DON'T THINK YOU'RE SAFE FROM ME WITH THAT NECKALCE! EVEN IF THE ONE YOU NICKNAMED SUSIE RESETS, I'LL MAKE THESE JUMPING TO CONCLUSIONS MORONS THINK **YOU** DID IT!" Envicha spits, he then turns back into a human. Angel comes to the rescue with Bar's notes from his pockets since Bartender is a bit spoked. Everyone now stares at Bartender. It was now or never. Bartender thought to himself for a moment, and comes to a conclusion. Even though he didn't have the up most confidence in himself, it was better than nothing.

"Alright, I will tell you who made the deal, and who actually killed Chicken," Bartender says. Envicha laughs, clearly confident that Bar will say the wrong answer.

"Bar…we already know who killed Chicken. It was Mob," Trash says.

"That's what you think, but the person who made the deal and killed Chicken are one in the same, and Mob wouldn't do that to himself. And well if he did, it would definitely not be in that way. Seriously, if it was…I doubt he would be able to sew his own eyes shut…" Bartender says.

"Excuse me, I saw another perdition, named Zinophobe, convince others to do exactly that. It…was disturbing," Envicha says, and then says to the fourth wall, "There's nothing to their name. Don't look it up. It's not a real word,"

"Well, get on with it! Who did it?" Scout says.

"Well first I need to know where Cop slept," Bartender says.

"3rd one down from the door," Cop says.

"No, you're right next to me…" Trash says. Bartender smiles as know he knows exactly what happened.

"I believe no, I am confident that it is…" Bartender says, "Cop!"

Chapter 14

"What!" Everyone except Bar say this.

"But Cop is a swell guy!" Trash says.

"He works in the police force for justice! He can't be a cold-blooded murderer!" Dr. Fully says.

"Did you hit your head on something?" Scout says.

"You think I, did it?" Cop says.

"I honestly thought you were going to say Scout," Envicha admits.

"What's going on-HEY!" Niko wakes up and then gets immediately knocked back unconscious by Envicha.

"Oops," Envicha says in a concern voice, that even a deaf olm could tell was fake.

Bartender is now feeling a bit uncertain of his choice now, but there is no going back now. He takes a breath, and explains:

"I want to get your attention to the dagger, Envicha destroyed. 1. Him destroying the dagger is an automatic give away that it is important. Not just some random dagger that just so happened to fall off Mob's body. It was found on Chickens body. Now, why would Mob stab Chicken's body?"

"Because he hated Chicken?" Trash says.

"But then it wouldn't be important enough to destroy. The answer is because of the method of murder. Mob **suffered** before he died…which means he didn't die instantly. Now what would you do if you were being murdered, besides escaping? Try to have justice! Mob might have known he wasn't going to get out of this so he threw a dagger at Chicken's body where it was found by my assistant, Angel," Bartender then pats Angel's head, "This was away to expose his killer for the rest of us…Now what would a dagger meant for killing help for finding his killer? Simple! Chicken was killed, so the dagger could mean that his killer and Chicken's murderer were one in the same,"

"Wow, and just from one dagger! No wonder you broke it!" Trash says to Envicha.

Bartender continues, "This means that the killer couldn't have been Dr. Fully, since he and Chicken were like brothers, and there was no way he would kill Chicken, even if he was in his way! Another piece of evidence of who it could be, is that Mob was innocent. If everyone remembers the night of Chicken's death, there were some odd sounds in the bunch. Two people leaving their rooms, and one person 'leaves' their room. Only one person comes back. There were no other murders except

Chicken's, at the time, and no one said they went into the bar.

Even if we assume one of us went somewhere else, they would

have only been able to go to someone else's room or the bar, and

then two people would verify each other's alibi, or be a witness.

Another reason, one of these people that 'left' their rooms was

very close to the door. It only takes 4 pats to make it to the door if

you were first, so it could only be Mob. However, there was a

delay. The sounds made it almost like someone came back into

the hallway, went into Mob's room, did something, and then

went back into the hallway, then into the bar. This something,

was planting the murder weapon to frame Mob,"

"That…makes sense," Trash says.

"Wait! We were wrong! Oh, I owe Mob an apology-Oh right.

Gosh, I'm a terrible person," Dr. Fully says.

"Congratulations, you're the last to know!" Scout says

sarcastically.

"Unfortunately, that doesn't narrow it down a whole lot.

Like Scout said, he's the only person who doesn't completely hate

Mob, but at the same time no one hated Chicken enough to kill

him, right? Well, like Envicha said, he'll kill anyone who get in

his way. So, why could it not be the same for his partner? This is

what I think happened: Chicken goes into the bar. The murderer

goes into the bar to have a talk with Envicha since his identity

was still unknown. The murderer sees Chicken, who is a variable

witness to his meeting. Since the logical thing to do would be tell

the others of a perdition, the murderer needed to get rid of

Chicken fast. They grabbed a stool, and swung it on Chicken's

head, which smashed his skull, and killed him instantly. They

then ordered, Envicha to clean it up, and hide the body upstairs.

The reason I think Envicha moved the body is because he is a professional. His job is to fulfil any desires his client has, which could be murder. The evidence for this is we found blood in the bar, while one stool was missing. The point is Chicken's body was taken care of. This murderer however, needed to get rid of the murder weapon, but he had a grudge against Mob so framing him was a logical step in his mind. This rules out Scout since he is neutral on everybody,"

"Not everybody, I think you suck," Scout says.

"I agree, Bartender sucks!" Envicha says.

"I'm literally telling everybody your innocent…Anyways, since Trash can't be the deal maker, as I stated before, I have now ruled out everybody except Cop who is the only person who came back. If you counted the two Rein's steps one came from Chicken's room, and the other from Cop's room. I know it's Cop's room since I ruled out Dr. Fully already! Also, Cop went back into Chicken's room, I have no idea why, but probably a failed

attempt to throw us off,"

"Yeah! I'm innocent!" Dr. Fully says.

"For a final nail in the coffin. Niko!" Bartender points to the

unconscious police officer, "The deal was centered around

parallel universes, and Niko is definitely not part of Susie's plan.

He was brought here by Envicha. Mob told me he heard some

dragging, which was Envicha bringing Niko here. Another

thing…Niko stated that he was surrounded by people from the

Coven Clan. Now only one of us is from the Coven Clan, and

even if this Rein wasn't our Mob, Niko would still be from a

universe that none of us are in. So, the deal was to kidnap Niko.

Or possibly more Niko's. This rules out Dr. Fully, Mob and Scout

since they have no connection to Niko. Trash is too in love with

his own Niko-"

"I'M NOT GAY! OR PAN!" Trash says.

"GET OUT OF THE CLOSET, ALL YOUR OTHER VERSIONS OF YOURSELF ARE OUT! YOU ARE PROBABLY THE ONLY ONE IN THE **MULTIVERSE** STILL IN THE CLOSET!" Envicha says.

"Anyways. Closet or not. I don't think Trash is a yandere, and he could've made the deal for his own Niko, but it wouldn't fit in an envy related sin. Lust perhaps," Envicha notably hisses at that "Once again, we are left with Cop as the only option. Cop was able to fake being sad since he's always sad! And if we going to address the open door, and the missing key. Cop has been exposed to criminals like Scout beforehand so it wouldn't be a complete stretch to say he knows how to pickpocket. Didn't it seem a bit strange that Cop suddenly hugged Dr. Fully out of nowhere?"

"Yeah, that was kind of strange. He was never the touchy feelings type of Rein," Dr. Fully says.

"Ok, what about my motive. You keep going back to envy, but what would I be envious of?" Cop says.

"Heh, glad you asked. Let me tell you a story. Once upon a time there was a Rein who was abused by his family. After he moved out, he became homeless, and fell deep in a rut. However, he met a kind, noble police officer named Niko. He offered this Rein a helping hand, and because of this he ended up joining the police force and became Niko's partner, instead of Richard, which made them close friends, if not perhaps even more. This job made him learn how to think like a criminal. However, disaster struck. They were sent on a mission to stop a Coven Clan attack; however, Niko heroically sacrificed his life to stop the clan. This Rein wanted to save his Niko's life, but he wasn't strong or perhaps not fast enough. Either way, Niko's life ends, and that was his only friend. That grief was crushing. It didn't help that he met an alternate version of himself that could travel freely across timelines, and that he was given a timeline hopper, where he learned about all these different timelines, and their living Niko's. He learned how most Reins didn't care for the police officer. He started thinking to himself, 'Why are these Reins not paying attention to Niko. He's the best! He's alive and well, why aren't they happy, that's a good thing! Why do they get to have Niko! *I cared* about my Niko, and they don't! **They don't deserve to have Niko. I do**.' This envious thought process, about how others had what he wanted, and took for granted drove him mad, which caused him to make a deal with a perdition. Now we are here today. As this person, who gives people with mental illness a bad name, stands before us. Let me ask you this…Was it worth it?"

Cop doesn't speak for a second, then laughs manically. Envicha turns into a snake and coils around him, not in a crushing type of way, but more of a protection way.

"You got it! I'm the killer. I'll admit it. I killed Chicken, and Mob! But what are you going to do about it?" Cop says giving off a creepy unhinged smile.

"We are going to take you down!" Trash says.

"Yeah!" Dr. Fully says.

"Eh, I'm in," Scout says.

Chapter 15

A fight breaks lose. Everyone tries to take down the shapeshifting perdition and the very skilled cop. Bartender tries fighting Envicha, since he's the only one who is protected against him; however, Bar is not protected against Cop, who grabs another stool and comes out of nowhere, and starts swinging at Bartender. Angel tries to help Bar, but is quickly knocked away by Envicha and then landing like bullet into Niko's forehead, who again just woke up. This causes both of them to fall unconscious. Envicha even though facing off three Reins at the same time seems to be winning. He is also focusing his attacks on Scout, of all people. Bartender assumes that Scout's Niko suffered a similar fate as Cop's Niko, so Cop is angry at Scout for not caring at all. Shivers went down Bar's spine, at the thought of not caring about his friend Niko, but it is short lived because of Cop trying to smash his skull in. Unfortunately for him, Cop is a cop, and Bartender is a bartender. So, Cop quickly overpowers him. He is standing on top of Bartender.

"You're an over worker, right? So, let this be a forced vacation…for all eternity," Cop says, and he then aims the stool for Bartender's head.

Bartender's life flashed before his eyes. He remembered the abuse his parents gave him, the decision to run away from that, the hopelessness he felt while homeless, that spark of determination and perseverance when he saw that tv show about how a millionaire came to be, him getting a job, learning how to be a bartender, making those business deals, eventually buying

that old run down building, him hiring Selvester and many

others, the many hours and services he provided for his bar,

getting that best bar reward, meeting Niko and Richard, meeting

the cultists, meeting Susie, seeing the cultists for what they really

were, getting renamed Bartender, meeting Angel, finding about

Chicken's death, defending Mob, almost being murdered by a

perdition only to be saved by Susie, finding out about Mob's

death, revealing who was the man behind the slaughter, and now

going to be murdered. Despite everything, Bartender lived a good

life. He didn't recognize what emotion was swamping over him.

Relaxed? Acceptance? Happy? Sad? Angry? Possibly a mix of all

them. There were some flaws. His self-hate, and his workaholic

tendencies got in the way of being happy, but he knew how to

move forward, unlike Cop. As soon as that stool hit his skull it

would be over, but he realized for the first time that he wasn't deserving of death. In an adrenaline filled rush, Bartender grabs the stool and throws it to the side. Then he punches the surprised Rein, and he falls to the floor. Cop gives him an angry glare, and then…nothing.

Cop freezes in place like a statue, and it isn't out of fear. Cop wiggles a bit like he's trying to get up. Bartender then realizes that just like Cop he couldn't move as well. Nobody could move. It seemed as if they were all put on pause. *Clap, Clap, Clap.*

"I think this experiment was a success," Susie says. She had appeared in the room, while Bartender had his life flash before his eyes.

"Oh, you. Why?! This literally how I can exist. Animals need to kill for food! I didn't do anything wrong!" Envicha says. He is the only one who can still speak; however, he still cannot move.

"Envicha, I can **tolerate** your behavior towards my world, but please don't involve timeline hopping. It gets bothersome real fast," Susie sighs.

"…" Envicha says pouting like a two-year-old. This immature nature was also shared by Susie, who is acting like she was a fake smarter, older sister. It is comforting to know, that God and a demon, who both could kill them all so easily, behaved like immature children.

"Anyways, I'm going to clean up this mess," Susie says. Cop suddenly vanishes, along with the stool.

"D-did y-you just snapped my client out of existence!" Envicha says.

"I teleported him to jail! You can't kill creations! Even if it's your own!" Susie sighs, but it seems she still wanted to kill him though.

"Why do you always say that like you are better than me, when you don't even see the living beings you created as equals?" Envicha says. Susie ignores what Envicha said.

"I now need you to sacrifice, Mob's soul," Susie says.

"…No,"

"For crying out LOUD! You have *plenty* of souls at your kingdom! Why can't you just spare literally one!"

"…Everyone else has better souls than me…"

Susie then screams at this rebuttal.

"Ugh fine…How about this. In your timeline, I believe Malrapture was never defeated," Susie says.

"That stupid Lust Perdition…"

"I know you aren't a wrath perdition, but wouldn't you want to have a little revenge? I know just the trick to help you, since Bartender's Malrapture has already been killed,"

"…I'm listening,"

"So just give me the soul, and break that Rein's deal. Then I can bring back those two Reins that died, and I will personally help you take revenge,"

"Yes, for the souls, but no for breaking the deal"

"What! Why won't you! It's just some rando. Betraying one person won't hurt!"

"I. AM. NOT. MAL.RAP.TURE!"

"…What would it be then, because I don't approve of this deal,"

"…How about this. That Niko, and all the others I captured can go free, and back to their timelines, in a week. Until then, they are going to be forced to hang out with Cop, and that one," Envicha looks at Bartender, "Will be mutilated, and killed in a horrible way in front of me…and Cop I supposed, and you can't bring him back until the week is over. Got it?"

Bartender's face lit up with fear and shock, and his expression was shared with the other Reins, even Scout.

"*Sigh* But they won't remember it, at least not Bartender. I still need to reward him for his cooperation. If that's set, then it's a deal,"

"Deal!"

Susie then approaches Bartender. He attempts to look up at Susie with an expression of 'What the #$@$!' but fails.

"Sorry about this, but don't worry it's a good ending! If I do decide for these morons to keep their timeline hoppers, they can tell you about how I resurrected those two Reins. Also, you won't remember a thing! Well about being killed that is…But if you don't remember. Did it technically happen?"

"Stop monologuing like super villain and get on with it!"

"Alright, alright. I'll do it,"

Suddenly, everything faded to black, and Bartender couldn't recall what happened next.

Chapter 16

Bartender wakes up back in his bed. He yawns and looks out his window and sees a morning in a bustling city. "Was it all a dream? That was some crazy dream" Bartender thinks to himself. He looks over and sees a yellow rat, looking exactly like Angel, sleeping on his nightstand. "Weird," He thinks to himself. He goes downstairs to clean his bar, which appears to be empty except for three people. He looks over to them and realizes they are a very worried Niko, Richard, and Selvester.

"I know those cultists did something to him!" Niko says.

"Niko calm down! We'll find him, I'm sure!" Richard says.

"We could just go and attempt to raid Coven Clan," Selvester states.

"Aw, your boyfriend…" Richard teases his brother.

"SHUT UP WE ARE JUST COWORKERS, AND I'M COMPLETELY STRAIGHT" Selvester says in an uncharacteristic denial tone.

"Richard, are you ready to help me take down the locked closet door that is your brother's denial of his sexuality," Niko says.

"Ready when you are," Richard says.

"Am I interrupting something?" Bartender asks.

"REIN!" The three men in the bar shout, and tackle hug him. It takes Bartender a moment to realize his name is back to being Rein, not Bartender.

"Where were you! I went into work, and you didn't even open up shop early!" Selvester says, and acts like not opening up the shop early was equal to an emergency. The worst part is that it is a very valid way of thinking towards Rein.

"Yeah! You were gone for over a week! We put up missing posters! We thought the Coven Clan kidnapped you!" Niko says.

"Yeah! We thought they try to torture you to learn your bartender secrets," Richard says. It is strange how Richard was worried about Rein, since they barely met, but then the realization strikes him. They share a mutual friend of Niko, and if Selvester did have a tiny crush on Rein; that would be another reason for his brother to help. So, if Niko and Selvester were worried then Richard was worried. That also proves that Niko thought Rein as a friend, which is nice. Wait a minute, they said he was gone for over a week…oh. Oh NO. The dream was real, and he was probably tortured for a yandere and a demon for a week. Fantastic. Thank ant- Susie that he didn't remember it. That reminds him, he's going to have to rethink his religion. Maybe become an atheist.

"Um, the real explanation is a bit too crazy right now. So, let's just say someone needed my help, and in doing so I had to spend a week somewhere else," Rein says.

The four of them talked about contacting other people about where you are going next time, and false promises that he won't do it again, because Rein isn't sure if Susie would like his help again, but he didn't really think he would like to help her again. For obvious reasons. They soon all went outside, talking about having to call off the search, and Rein looking up at the sky, smiling about his life choices, and how great he is.

Epilogue

A month after the events of what happened, Rein meets up with the cultists again, because they all needed time to recover from what had happen. Especially after he told Niko, that they aren't in fact Coven Clan members, and the dangerous one is no longer part of the group. Apparently, after the week was up, Envicha took Cop's soul, which caused his life to end. The other Reins then tell him what happened after everything went black. So, Susie did in fact resurrect Chicken and Mob. However, they didn't go to the same afterlife, Susie wasn't kidding when perditions take anyone's who was involved soul. So, not only did Mob have a horrible death, since both Reins seem to remember their death, he spent an hour in what was basically hell. He needed therapy. Chicken is mostly alright, but he seems a bit jumpier. Dr. Fully started trying to learn about mental illness and grief, so he can help those people not turn into Cop, and Trash was helping with the same goal in mind. Scout decides to change his life around.

Finally, everyone agrees, the best/only good part of that whole misadventure was that they were now able to show id to Bartender so they can all have drinks, and Bartender can now get paid for their drinking habits.

Acknowledgements

- Me for thinking this stupid idea in the first place and writing it

- My aunt who wanted me to write a murder mystery, who still can't read it until she finishes beta reading something else

- Mom, Dad, and Ruth for helping me edit it

- Puffballs United for making a very enjoyable game series that I will use as inspiration for other projects.

- Word Documents so I am able to actually write this stuff down, and have spell check! Whoopie!

- Krita for the cover